MUDDY WATERS

High Hills Publishing LLC

Muddy Waters

Chrys Brobbey

Dedicated to:

All those who strive to make the world
a better place for the benefit of humanity.

This book contains 2 stories:

Muddy Waters

Twist of Fate

Muddy Waters

Prelude:

This humorous story of the odyssey of a personified unit of currency is a satirical rendition. It captures the foibles of an actual society, here represented by an imaginary country. The observations mirror the practices that prevail in many other societies, and are thought provoking to raise questions about issues that seem normal or have been taken for granted. The logic is to stir the *'muddy waters'* of society to perhaps stab the public conscience at a reawakening and reformation.

Vivid descriptions immerse the reader right into the action: from politicians who are deluded to believe they are in public service to cater to their inflated egos, to moonshine addicts who consider the self-sentence of death as fair bargain for their pleasures.

Valuable lessons, as well as much food for thought, will linger in the mind of the reader well beyond the pages of this book.

Chapter 1

Charm at the Bank

The intensity of the light hits me like a bolt of lightning as the bundle of notes is lifted out of the drawer. I lie at the top of the pack, whether by chance or privilege. It is steamy at the Shika Commercial Bank, Amet Market Branch, all inspite of the humming heavy-duty air-conditioner. What with the many people in the bank, and the sun burning with ferocity this noon in the city on the equator.

By contrast it had been cozy and cool in the drawer. The drawer had been occupied by many currency notes of my kind and others in bundles. Each time the drawer opened, a slender hand dipped in and out went one or more bundles. At other times wads dropped in.

While in the drawer I could not see the outside, but I heard people talking from time to time with the teller. That is how come I know her name is Cherita. A sweet French sounding name laced with meaning. She has a sweet and tantalizing voice, and she is always patient with customers. The customer is always right, they say. But Cherita invariably manages to come out right by getting an irate customer to calm down. I fantasize about seeing her face. I imagine her smile, hopefully exposing a set of milky teeth concealed behind luscious painted lips.

I am not let down. When I become accustomed to the light I behold Cherita's face. She spots a cute smile as she extends a long slender hand and offers the bundle to the customer behind the counter. He's a gentleman, resplendent in a three-piece suit, even on this hot afternoon. Clearly a successful businessman, he's all smiles as he looks Cherita directly in the face with flirtatious interest. He is oblivious to all the bustle of activity in the hall, as he is mesmerized by the bulging brown eyes set in the sculpted round face. Time stands still for the enchanted customer as he literally devours pretty Cherita with enthusiastic eyes.

People come and go, and bank officials attend to eager customers in glass cubicles. The dispenser in the corner spits out cool dark thick liquid cocoa as a lady customer works at the mechanism. A male client sits on a couch, patiently nursing a cup of the cocoa beverage, as he waits his turn to consult with a customer representative. The beep of his cell phone startles him and he spills some of the liquid as he sets the cup down. He begins to speak to an invisible audience, and hurries out of the banking hall as his tone rises.

All these happenings are at the blind side of my fellow notes that are not privileged to be at the top of the bundle.

At last the bundle changes hands, from pretty Cherita to the customer. The smitten businessman hangs on as he pulls out a wallet and extracts a card and hands it over to her, with a generous tip.

I'm one of the currency notes referred to as the "Zolar" used as money in the Republic of Shika, on the continent of Africa. Red in color, I bear on my front the images of the founding fathers of the country. They were the architects of political independence from the colonial master, her Majesty the Queen's Great Britain. The country was then known as the Green Coast.

On my back is the picture of the hydroelectric dam. The dam provides light to the towns and cities, and power for the industries in the country. The construction of the dam led to the creation of the largest man-made lake in the world. It stands as a proud distinction for the country.

Amongst other features I bear the legend 'Z1'. That Idicates my value as 'One Zolar' note. There are other notes in denominations of 2, 5, 10, 20, 50 and 100. However, there are more of my kind and by far widespread in terms of circulation than any of the others, and this fact boosts my ego a great deal.

He shifted his focus from the floor to me. "I was a drowning man and I held on to the straw that floated my way," he said.

"It's now time to let go of the straw and take hold of something more tangible," I said. "You can make a much better living if you want to take my offer to engage in selling the second-hand clothing in the packages here."

Mr. Menach shot up from his seat. "You mean you brought these just for me?" he asked. "But I don't have the money to pay for them."

"Please take your seat," I told him. "No need for cash up front. You sell the items; keep the profit; remit me the principal to repurchase for you fresh stocks."

"I can help with the selling," his wife, Clara, volunteered. "It sells like hot cake here in the village when the traders bring them on market days. On other days we travel to towns close by to buy when we need any."

I was pleased by her enthusiasm which proved to be infectious on her hesitant husband. By the mathematics of affordability most people had to make do with the second-hand clothing. The import, wholesale and retail of the used clothing was a flourishing trade throughout the country. The few local apparel manufacturing companies complained of lack of patronage due to the influx of the cheaper imports. Some of the companies even folded up as a result. But there was no end in sight for the widespread trade even though the affected interest groups lobbied for a legislation to embargo the imports on hygienic grounds, if not for the protection of the local industry and jobs. But the bulk of the populace depended on it to the extent that any regime that dared to prohibit it risked a trashing at the next elections.

"Thank you for caring about me," my former head-teach complimented. "Between me and Clara we can make a success of it." His wife's passion had in deed acted like an elixir on him.

I reached into my pocket and pulled out a bulging envelope. "This is for you." I extended my hand towards him. "Here is some money to cover your needs between now and when you can draw from your profits."

He hesitated to take the envelope from me. "No, that is going too far," he protested. "We shall manage in the interim."

"Please, take it," I said and placed the envelope on his laps. "Consider it as a loan to be repaid when you are in the position to do so." I reasoned that he needed the money if he did not have to continue trading in palm-wine before they could fall on the profits from the sale of the clothing. Offering the money as a loan and not for gratis not only made its acceptance easier but would induce them to work harder to be able to repay. But in reality I was not counting on taking it back.

With a pair of scissors I cut open one of the bales of clothing and emptied the contents on the floor. The items comprised miscellaneous clothing for both sexes of all ages. They looked neat and reasonably new for used articles.

The methodology I outline was for Mr. Menach to make an inventory list by recording in a notebook each item of clothing and the price at which it could be sold. I suggested that the prices be set below what competitors charged in order to attract more customers to make quick turnovers. After that he was to sum up the inventoried prices and compare to the cost as per the tag on the bale. That could be a painstaking exercise, but not as arduous as the production and sale of palm-wine. Clara seemed to easily grasp the procedure in spite of her lack of schooling. Apparently she was under tutoring in literacy by her husband. It seemed that with their corroboration in the new venture her learning would be accelerated with the husband having more time to devote to teaching her. I assured them of continuity in supply of stocks so long as they fulfilled their part of the bargain. Our discussions continued with Clara's full participation till all the pertinent issues were ironed out. In the end I was satisfied that prospects for Mr. Lionel Menach's fiscal wellbeing and redeeming his esteem were bright. I could already picture him in his former position of head-teacher as the joie de vivre repossessed him. A sudden transformation seemed to have come over him. He appeared buoyed up in spirit. No longer would he be obsessed with suicidal thoughts or wish for a calamitous happenstance to end his life.

But it was sad to speculate as to how many of his kind had actually carried out their suicidal intentions due to betrayal and neglect by the society for which they had devoted their services. And the question was how many more would travel that path unless the powers that be awoke from their power-seduced apathy?

Insensitivity needed to give way to empathy. Official actions and policies had to be weighed on the scale of fairness and their consequences on people. The divide between sanity and insanity was thread thin, and insensitivity the sharp scalpel that easily severed it.

Twist 5

It was a little over three weeks after my return to the city from my trip of redemption to the village. My conscience no longer plagued me on the matter of Mr. Menach, my former head-teacher. I had done for him what the government failed to do. It was up to him and the wife to rise to the challenge. And I had the conviction that they were more than capable. I had no worries on the matter.

Therefore when I picked from my letterbox the envelope bearing Mr. Lionel Menach's return address I expected nothing but good news. But I was mistaken. The letter, written a week earlier, was in his noted neat handwriting and flowing scholastic Queen's English. It seemed that his absence from the classroom for so long had not impacted negatively on his intellectual talent. I read the first two sentences whilst still standing before I realized I needed to rely on my coach like a vehicle on rough terrain would depend on its shock absorbing mechanism. Seated, I took in a deep breath, held onto it for some five seconds before exhaling and then started to read again from the beginning:

Dear Mr. Zac Brown,

To go straight to the point I wish to apprise you of the woes that descended upon us in the aftermath of your well-intentioned visit over two weeks ago. The presence of your pristine car parked by my house had not gone unnoticed by the faceless criminals who prowl by day and strike by night. On the very day of your departure they descended upon us close to midnight. They took the three bales of clothing and the envelope with the money and left only when they thought I and Clara were dead from their fistic display of sadism. Fortunately both of us were only unconscious when we were discovered in the morning. Since then we have been on admission at the government hospital in the regional capital recuperating. I am now strong enough to write to you. Clara is also recovering fast. The doctor caring for us assures us that no vital parts of our bodies have been seriously affected, which we consider a divine miracle.

The silver lining in the clouds is that out of the blue my four long-lost children came to see me here at the hospital. Somehow one of them got to hear of the incident and informed the others. They are of course all now grown-ups and I am grateful to my former wife for taking good care of them, though I wish she had not taken them away with her when she decided to decamp. Unfortunately I am told she departed this world some five years ago, and I can only hope that she is resting in peace. I bear my children no grudge for not making contact with me earlier, for erring is associated with immaturity and forgiveness with maturity.

And now I come to the main substance of my letter. They say God works in mysterious ways, but I do not believe that God approved of the event that landed us here in the hospital. But the twist of fate of my regaining consciousness and the commercial on the national lottery airing on the TV in my room at the same time could not be by mere coincidence. The information that the jackpot amount had soared to 500 million Zollars was to me irresistibly tempting even in my hazy state of mind. The nurse attending to me was reluctant but I persisted. In the end she yielded, fearing I might get out of bed and venture across the street, an act that could lead to her being fired. The Z5 bill that I had taken out of the envelope with the money you lent me was still intact in the pocket of the pair of shorts that I was wearing when they brought me to the hospital. The nurse promptly returned from the corner shop with the ticket bearing 5 lines of auto-pick wager. She said it was a waste of a sick man's money as I folded the ticket and stuck it into my pocket.

Let me say that I do not know what compelled me to insist on the nurse procuring the ticket for me, other than the commercial referred to earlier. I have never been a lottery fan or addict, but the urge was compulsive this time like a surge of an electric current leading me into the gamble for the first time. But it turned out to be a propitious move, or call it the beginner's luck, for I hit the jackport against the odds of one chance in a billion. Or it could be that the nurse who grudgingly abandoned her duties to get me the ticket is a lucky girl with the touch of Midas. I have not told her or anyone else yet. Not even Clara who is in a different ward, fearing that she might go again into a swoon, this time through shocked excitement.

Surely, all's well that ends well. The strange turn of fate that brought us to the hospital without doubt began as a tragedy, but the denouement portends nothing but the opposite, a hundred-and-eighty degree counter traverse. To quote from Katty Macane: *"There's a silver lining to every cloud that sails about the heavens if we could only see it."*

It is also said that *"he who laughs last, laughs best"*. I believe I'll now have the last laugh over fate and the insensitive officials who have caused me so much suffering in the past. But I owe everything to you as the faithful messenger in this twist of fate.

It is a week since the draw and they are looking for the winner to show up. I read that in the popular newspaper today. I trust you. I want you to come for the ticket to claim the prize. You are the genesis to the windfall and you must consider yourself prominent in the scheme of affairs. The nurse with the touch of Midas will also be well rewarded.

When you come we shall have more to talk about, but do well to come soon as the ticket is burning holes in my pocket. Will you?

Your former Head-teacher,
Lion Menach
Lionel Menach.

Twist 6

The letter slipped out of my fingers. It lay on the floor smiling back at me as I sat shaking in the couch, my face plastered in a wide smile. I steadied my excitation to avert a heart attack. I did not know if the message was the reality or a yarn. Hastily hauling the heap of old newspapers from the book shelf I fumbled through with fevered urgency. I found the edition I was searching for and cruised through the pages looking at the headings. I found it on the back page, almost when I was about to give up.

"**Biggest Ever Jackpot Prize Won**," the caption read. It was a long article, so I skimmed over to the relevant portion that read:

"The winning ticket was bought in Kumass at the Quinzo Mart right across from the government hospital. The lucky winner is yet to come forward to claim the prize. There is a sixty-day grace period after which the prize will be forfeited to the state if not claimed."

That was all I was looking for, so I read no further.

Instantly I transitioned to the image of me holding the big dummy check at the presentation ceremony. I had an expansive grin as the cameras flashed from all angles. It was the smile that would be translated onto many other faces with the utmost largess at my command. The kind of sunny smile that I read in the expressions of my ex-head-teacher and his pretty wife when I gave the bales of clothing and the cash-studded envelope to them. Now they were in the position to create similar smiles on the faces of the masses of people caught in poverty as they formerly were.

But first I needed to get going to make that life-changing journey to the hospital to collect the ticket. Imagine that small slip of paper holding the key to life-infusing millions of dough like a deluge on drought-harassed California. The engine of my car purred to life with unusual enthusiasm. As I drove along the whole world seemed to smile at me. There was even laughter in the wind that swirled around. The chirping of the birds that floated through the air sounded like a chorus of angels from on high. The gas pedal seemed to operate on its own without my having to step on it, like it was in auto mode. I was in auto mode myself, on cloud nine as the car hurtled along. Even the bumpy roads seemed to have become smooth. Or was it the shock absorbers that could now withstand the knocks with unusual gallantry?

But wait a minute! Not that I lacked money. But was the abundance of it now going to have a meaningful impact on my life? It depended upon how I handled it; the perspective from which I viewed it.

I still kept my focus on the road, and my driving reflexes alert. But my thoughts were in overdrive mulling over money matters, recollecting the opinions of others on money. Foremost was God, whose view mattered most: *"For the love of money is a root of all kinds of evil. Some people, in their eagerness to get rich, have wandered away from the faith and caused themselves a lot of pain."* (1Timothy 6:10).

It was not money per se that was evil, but the *love* of it that led people to seek to acquire it through harmful means.

The O'Jays elaborated on it in a song:

> *"For the love of money*
> *People will steal from their mother*
> *People will rob their own brother*
> *People can't even walk the street*
> *People will lie, Lord they will cheat*
> *People don't care who they hurt or beat*
> *Money can drive people out of their minds*
> *Don't let, don't let, don't let money rule you*
> *People don't let money change you."*

God wanted us to have money as per His promises, notably amongst them: *"And I will give you the treasures of darkness, and hidden riches in secret places..."* (Isaiah 45:3)

Accordingly God endowed individuals and nations with treasures beneath and above the earth: gold, silver, diamond, granite, coal, limestone, waters, forests, produce, animals, oil, etcetera. And above all He gifted humans with innate potentials and wisdom, and spirituality over and above money.

But God commanded that *"those who are rich in this present world not to be arrogant nor to put their hope in wealth, which is so uncertain, but to put their hope in God, who richly provides us with everything for our enjoyment."* (1 Timothy 6:17).

And further *"to do good, to be rich in good deeds, and to be generous and willing to share. In this way they will lay up treasure for themselves as a firm foundation for the coming age, so that they may take hold of the life that is truly life."* (1Timothy 6:18-19).

My resolve was to be "rich in good deeds" through the opportunity offered by the windfall. I needed to psyche myself into the willingness to share mood before all that much money came into our possession. For money could become a curse instead of a blessing: *"You say, 'I am rich; I have acquired wealth and do not need a thing.' But you do not realize that you are wretched, pitiful, poor, blind and naked."* (Rev 3:17). Money became a mammon to worship if it was hoarded, instead of giving to nurture a spirit of generosity.

Looking at the dashboard I realized that I was running low on gas. But that was nothing to worry about because the next refueling station was just a few miles distant. The question on my mind then was: what were some of the opinions of men on money, and were they in accord with biblical views?

Mark Twain was of the opinion that *"The lack of money is the root of all evil."*
In so much as money was essential for human survival, the lack of it endangered life, and could lead people to resort to foul means to acquire money. Starvation, diseases, crime, misery and early death were associated with the lack of money.

These are the more valid reasons that those blessed to have money in abundance give some to those who are unfortunate enough to lack for it. The generation of money is dependent on society as a whole, as a Robinson Crusoe existence cannot make one rich no matter how enterprising he may be. Logically, therefore, the Bill Gates, Warren Buffets, Mark Zukerbergs and others of their ilk have been spreading their largess to the benefit of society as a whole
. My intention was to follow in their steps with the lottery windfall. After all, it was the collective contribution of a group in society that was being entrusted into our care.

As noted by Aristotle Onasis, one of the richest men ever, *"After a certain point, money is meaningless. It ceases to be the goal."* My belief, therefore, was that the goal was to spread the money like wind-dispersed pollen grains over fertile lands to bear much fruit.

In the words of Pablo Picasso: *"I'd like to live as a poor man with lots of money."* This implied living a life of modesty and humility, which was the course I intened to follow inspite of my soon-to-be status as a nouveau millonaire. For it must be noted that money was not the all and everything in life. Flesh and blood would not change into steel and grit by the gaining of monetary wealth. The common denominator amongst all of humanity, rich or poor, was their mortality. For as noted by Clifford Odets: *"Life shouldn't be printed on dollar bills."* For if it were so life would be relegated to the status of commerce instead of a breath of divinity.

But did I have any qualms about the practice of lottery itself? Suffice it to say that the pros and cons have been debated for centuries, ever since lots were cast by the Roman soldiers over who got to receive the seamless garment of the crucified Jesus, as recorded in John chapter 19 verse 24a: *"So they said to one another, Let us not tear it, but let us cast lots to decide whose it shall be."*
Earlier in Psalm 22:18 it was prophesied: *"They divide my garments among them, and for my clothing they cast lots."*
The epic book based on that lottery event, *"The Robe"* by Lloyd C. Douglas, relates how the soldier who won the cast attained salvation through the possession of the garment. In that wise the *lottery* served him a good purpose in that it led him to believe in Jesus as the Savior. Similarly, those who won in the myriad of lotteries, all things being equal, should attain material improvement in their lives.

The lotteries are sanctioned by countries and the states to serve the purposes of the organizers and stakers. Revenues accrue to states and federal governments for their programs. It has spawned millionaires, but not known to have created any bankruptcies. In a sense it can be likened to the various insurance schemes like health, property or car insurance to which many subscribe but only a few cash out.

On the scale of ethics the lottery surely would not outweigh the sale of cigarettes and alcohol which rather wreak havoc on consumers' health and exact a toll on the medical and human resources of nations.

To stretch it further, the game of lottery can be likened to the activities of the host of political candidates who compete for the spoils of national offices during election cycles. In the words of the American poet, philosopher and author, *Henry David Thoreau: "All voting is a sort of gaming, like checkers or backgammon, with a slight moral tinge to it, a playing with right and wrong."* Like the few elite politicians who compete for positions through money-intensive campaigning, a vast number of the masses pitch in their widows' mites on tickets in the hope of winning jackpots. Many of the stakers see that as the only legitimate option available to them in the pursuit of changing their lives for the better. Desperation fuels their optimism of overcoming the overwhelming odds against winning in any kind of lottery. Their hopes for a possibly better life are renewed each time with the purchase of a ticket, however elusive and for how long. It acts as an elixir for continued existence, a boundless exercise of faith and hope for the future. It offers only a faint glimmer of hope, but hope nonetheless the way a drowning person will grab at a straw. Such hopefulness is reinforced whenever someone beats the odds, as happens on a regular basis to one or more of the millions of patrons. Every win shows that acing the odds is not a myth, leading every staker to believe that it is only a matter of time for his or her turn at winning. They are stubborn optimists, but not delusional. They exhibit the characteristic virtue of the vulture: *patience.* The close to thirty different species of vulture is one of the few types of birds found all over the world on almost every continent. Similary, the lottery phenemonon is endemic throughout the world as almost every country seeks to pinch cents and pennies from its citizens the way the vulture clean picks carrion one bite at a time. The adverising of tantalizing jackpots feeds the passion and greed of lottery stakers and non-stakers alike. It was one such promotion that had gotten my former headteacher hooked, and incredibly he had hit the jackpot on his first attempt. The twist of fate in his life had turned full cycle: from rags to riches, from grass to grace.

Lost in my thoughts I almost overshot the entrance to the gas station. I pulled in close to the service point and uncorked the tank cover. The gas surged through the hose into the tank whilst I stood guard. I was waiting for the automatic shut-off to indicate that the tank was full.

The battered car that turned into the station coughed and came to a stop short of the next filling point close to where I stood. Seconds later the engine wailed but failed to start. The driver got out and approached me. He looked as equally shabby as his car, but obviously younger than me.

"Excuse me, sir," he hailed me. "Can you give me a push?" He withdrew back to his car and stuck a hand through the window to direct the steering while at the same time pushing with the other hand. But the car did not budge, being slightly inclined uphill. I joined him and exerted a push on the trunk. The car moved slowly into position by the pump.

"Thank you, sir," he said as I walked back to my vehicle.

While I was in the process of capping my tank cover he looked in my way and said hesitantly: "Errrr, sir, can you help me fill up?" He had uncapped his car's tank cover and was in the process of dislodging the filling hose from the stand pump.

"That's quite easy," I replied. "You don't need any help in doing that."

"Errr....ooh," he stuttered. "I mean can you lend me your credit card?"

That was unexpected; like a jab to the groin.

I opened my mouth to question him further, but remembered just in time and swallowed my unuttered words of protest. Here was the biblical test to me as stated in 1Timothy 6.17-19: *"Instruct those who are rich in this present world not to be conceited or to fix their hope on the uncertainty of riches, but on God, who richly supplies us with all things to enjoy. Instruct them to do good, to be rich in good works, to be generous and ready to share. Storing up for themselves the treasure of a good foundation for the future, so that they may take hold of that which is life indeed."*

I went over and inserted my card into the payment slot. The liquid started to gush through the line into his tank. The beneficiary shot me a look of appreciation and relief that went right through me like the gas going through the hose.

"Just one gallon will do," he said. "I live close by."

"Let the tank fill up," I said. "It might come in useful."

Again that look of appreciation, mingled with surprise this time. It went through me once again like a hot knife through butter. At that point the money being drained in the form of fuel off my credit card was meaningless. Money had ceased to be the concern, replaced by the joy infused into the recipient, who appeared to be experiencing hard times.

"Awesome!" he said, as the click indicated that the tank was full. "You are an angel."

"Angels reside in the heavens, not here on earth," I pointed out to him.

"Yes," he agreed. "But God sometimes send them on errands to answer the prayers of us humans when we are in need. You've made my day, and strengthened my faith. Thank you, and stay blessed."

Stay blessed indeed, I reflected. All my life to date I had basked in showers of blessings. Many more people needed such blessings that I had enjoyed, as promised by God: *"Beloved, I wish above all things that you prosper and be in good health, even as your soul prospers."* (3 John 1:2). It was not that I merited those blessings, but I took God at His words and claimed the promised blessings.

When my new friend and beneficiary touched the ignition the refueled car roared to life with a vengeance. The engine seemed not to be as bad as the car looked on the outside. I waited for him to drive off before I was composed enough to resume my journey. The encounter of simply parting with a few bucks to help someone in need had been an stimulating experience for me altogether. Not that this was novel to me, but in that I was now certainly in the position to do that more often and liberally.

Surely it was going to be a new experience altogether for my former head-teacher and his wife; in their new roles to be possibly regarded as angels sent by God in response to people's prayers. My chance encounter to be of help to someone in need had been the momentum and the twists in a life changing saga beyond my wildest imagination. But imagine all peoples of the world living life in riches not by winning the elusive lottery, but through fairness and justice and the equitable distribution of wealth and opportunities. To quote John Lennon "**You may say I am a dreamer but I am not the only one.**"

So just begin to imagine!

THE END.

Other books by the author:

Life's Twists and Turns

(https://www.createspace.com/4294776)

Synopsis

Call it the drama of the prodigal son in reverse. Flamboyant Maulus Shane exudes chic and charm in social circles in his hometown Dorros, in the Republic of Zollara on the sunny continent of Africa. While he splurges his wealth to indulge his fantasies and pleasures he unconscionably abandons his son, Johan, to uncertain fate at the tender age of twelve.

Some years later the senile and diseased Maulus sets out to seek the now prosperous son in his time of adversity. The puzzle is how will Johan welcome the prodigal father whom he least expects to ever encounter face to face?

Complicating the issue is Johan's own search for answers to the unresolved cold-blooded murder of his beloved mother years ago, for which the father possibly holds the key. Will father and son each receive closure from the other through their mutual needs?

There is the benign uncle, Peter Shane, who bridges the gap between father and son in lives interweaved by twists and turns like a meandering forest path. He harbors an agonizing secret that yearns to be exorcised, but at the risk of dreadful consequences.

The shocking climax catches both the reader and protagonists unawares.

Chapter One (extract):

He stood shakily on tired numbed legs that threatened to collapse under him any moment. Not knowing the next step in his odyssey of uncertainty he stared at his new surroundings as if hypnotized. The hustle and bustle of the mass of humanity like a beehive at peak season was something altogether alien to him. A phalanx of people shouting out in multiple languages made the landscape resemble a re-enactment of the drama of the Tower of Babel. The blare of the sirens of an assortment of vehicles maneuvering for space comingled in a bedlam of an erratic orchestra. Sounds booming from giant juke boxes advertising the most recent hot musical releases assaulted his ears like a hammer to the anvil. More buses kept arriving discharging passengers like ships jettisoning cargo into troubled seas.

Maulus Shane had finally arrived at the main bus terminal in Aurela, the capital city of the Republic of Zollara. It had seemed like centuries travelling in the old bus on tortuous roads over the three-hundred mile journey. There had been hardly any room to stretch his legs and he had felt pains whenever he tried to move them around.

That was his first time coming to the city in the sixty-five years of his existence. Once upon a time he had lived in prosperity and in comfort in his hometown, Dorros. There had been no reason for him to travel out, either for tourism or out of necessity. He had been a prosperous tycoon then. But aging and bad lifestyle choices had exposed him to sicknesses and adversities that had eroded his physical strength and wealth. The vicissitudes in the tides of life had conspired with fate and character foibles to render him a shadow of his former self.

He still recalled with nostalgia the good times, when he had been lord of all that he surveyed and stood tall like the legendary Colossus of Rhodes. But now compelling need had driven him like a wounded lion out of its den in search of rescue. His need for assistance was urgent, but prospects of redemption unsure.

The smell of the variety of foods sold openly at the station stung his nostrils. It awakened the awareness of hunger gnawing at his innards. The journey had taken over ten hours. And though the bus had made stops at rest spots along the route he had not been in the mood to refresh himself. He had been lost in introspection; recollections that evinced only regrets upon regrets upon regrets.

How could he, the once mighty Maulus Shane, have fallen so low? Harassing guiltiness over a lifetime of debauchery had become the albatross around his neck that weighed heavily upon him. Unlike the driver at the controls of the aged vehicle who had steered him and his fellow passengers safely over the long journey, he had navigated his life into a ditch of deep gloominess. Character was the steering-wheel to the human machinery just as a rudder was to a ship; the lack of which led to disastrous consequences. He had lacked character while swimming in a life of wealth as long as the wealth lasted. And now he was reaping the drawbacks.

Maulus remembered a classic favorite saying of the head-teacher of the basic school he attended up to primary six, which was the highest level of education he attained. The educator had drawn attention so persistently to the quotation from T. S. Elliot's book 'Murder in the Cathedral' that it got imbedded into the receptive minds of allthe pupils in the school. And like a leech burrowed deep into the skin of an unwilling host it had stayed with him. It had been like music in perpetual play echoing and re-echoing within him:

"Only the fool, fixed in his folly, may think
he can turn the wheel on which he turns."

He realized he had played the fool all along, thinking he could turn the wheel of life. It was like a child on a high merry-go-round at the backyard playground seeking to paddle the rotations with his feet like he would bicycle pedals. Through irresponsibility he had 'murdered' himself in the bedrooms and pubs of his town Dorros and the nearby towns. Someone had advised of the need to bid goodbye to regrets to free oneself of the 'weigh-down' effects of chewing on regrets. But how could he do so when the results of his deeds followed him doggedly like a faithful dog at the heels of its master?

When Maulus could no longer suppress the cravings of hunger he ambled over to the nearest food seller and bought a loaf of bread sandwiched with cheese and corned beef. He gobbled it down, swatting at the many hungry swooping flies that competed with him over the food. Finished, he gulped down some ice-cold water that made him wince in pain as the chill penetrated his decayed aching teeth.

Realizing the need to get moving, he asked the food seller for directions. She told him to move over to the section of the terminus where taxis picked passengers to the various suburbs of the city. He dragged himself on painful legs to the taxi arena. The cab drivers were shouting out location names as passengers boarded. Not knowing which of the locations was his intended destination Maulus stood by, confused. After a while he pulled out a piece of crumbled paper from his pocket and approached a driver who was busily canvassing for passengers. The driver took a look at the address on the paper and seemed to think for a time. Meanwhile the last passenger boarded the taxi-cab and it was time for the driver to move. He handed the slip of paper to the driver who was in line behind him. The new driver moved his taxi cab forward to the spot just vacated and opened the front passenger door for Maulus to enter. The old man shuffled over and lowered himself into the seat by the driver, relieved to take the weight off his weary legs. The chauffeur turned to Maulus who sat with quiet unease beside him and said in one of the local languages:

"Do you want me to take you to this address?"

Maulus did not understand the dialect used by the driver, and told him so in English.

There were about ninety different tribal groups living in the ten regions of the Republic of Zollara. There were as many lingos as the number of tribes and it was always guesswork knowing the dialect a person spoke. On casual encounters, people would try the use of their own vernacular first, and then change to the use of English if the other person did not speak the same lingua franca. English was the official language used in the Republic, and it was understood by almost all the citizens. It was the unifying element amongst the diverse tribal groups in a country that had been welded into a single entity by the departed British colonialist. But in reality the nation remained and functioned like a patchwork of quilted fabrics easily breakable at the seams; often evidenced by the inter-ethnic internecine conflicts.

The driver translated into English what he had said in his local tongue. Maulus nodded assent, and the driver told him the fee for a 'chartered ride.' The old man hesitated as the fare quoted was much more than the amount of money he had on him. Sensing his confusion the driver suggested a cheaper alternative. He could ride on the taxi that travelled the route of the suburb and alight at a point closer to his destination. The driver took Maulus to another taxi that had three passengers already seated. He showed the slip with the address to the other driver and gave the paper back to Maulus. The new driver indicated to Maulus to take the vacant seat at the back, and moved off as soon as he had slammed the door closed. Maulus fumbled with the seatbelt and managed to buckle up. Gloomy uncertainty etched over his bony and haggard face making him oblivious to the progress of the journey.

As he went along the driver could see Maulus, who was seated directly behind him, through the driving mirror. From the address shown him he knew which point along the route to make him alight. Then the old man would have to walk about half a mile to reach his destination. He was about the same age as his father, and he felt sorry for him on account of his frail appearance. He wished he could divert his course to take him to the address shown him. But there were difficulties: the other passengers would be taken off course from their drop off points; the road system was such that access to the address involved a circuitous route; also he would be behind time and lose his position in the loading queue at the end station. In the taxi business where there were more operators than the passenger demand justified, it was often difficult to achieve the daily sales target. There were good days and bad days, and the drivers had learnt to use the good days to offset the bad days. That made it difficult to do favors, no matter one's generous inclination.

It was with much reluctance therefore that the driver pulled up at a spot on the route and told the old man that was the point for him to alight. He declined to take the fare, and exiting the car he walked with Maulus across to the other side of the busy four-lane street.

Standing by the side of the busy road Maulus cast puzzled glances as cars whizzed by behind him. He could not help wondering why so many cars passed by but he was the solitary human pedestrian. He was grateful to the kind taxi driver who had taken time to guide him across the road when there was a lull in the traffic. It would have been a challenge to him to cross the road since his failing sight could not see far and wide.

He fished out of the pocket of his wrinkled pair of khaki pants the scrap of paper with the house address. He had never been to visit his son who lived there, and they had not seen each other for so many years that it could pass for eternity. They had been as distant in terms of relating to each other as the three hundred miles that separated them physically. The address had been given to him by his son's only friend in the hometown with whom the son kept contact. He had had to promise that he would not reveal the source. Much as he tried the friend would not give him his son's telephone number, claiming that he did not have it. He could not fault him; he himself was to blame for not maintaining contact with his son during his hey days.

His son was not expecting his out of the blue visit. But it was a matter of life and death, and his son could be his only hope of redemption.

After what passed for eternity in time he saw a young boy coming in his direction. The boy was juggling a soccer ball, occasionally throwing it into the air and intercepting it with the head on its return downwards to fall some paces ahead of him. Maulus contemplated the scene with envy and nostalgia. He was once like that boy; youthful, comely, energetic, happy-go-gay. It was great to be young then, and he had nursed many hopes, including becoming a soccer genius of the stature of the renowned Pelé do Nascimento of Brazil, or

Diego Armando Maradona of Argentina. Soccer was the sporting passion in the Republic of Zollara, talked about with regard to soccer as the Brazil of Africa. Every male youth in the country dreamed of becoming a soccer star and player for the national team, the Saturn Angels, at the FIFA World Cup. Good players were quickly poached by renowned teams like Chelsea, Leeds, Manchester, Milan, Olympique Marseille, Bayern Munich and Barcelona. Such lucky players earned millions in Pounds Sterling, Liras, Francs and Deutsch Marks. They became the nouveau riche overnight and objects of admiration and envy throughout the republic. Their identifying hallmarks were the imposing mansions and luxury cars that they acquired overnight, and their conspicuous display in social circles of elegance and allure. Nurturing a soccer prodigy was the fantasy and prayer of every expectant mother. It was believed that the baby who emerged from the womb crying and kicking held the promise for a blossoming soccer career.

But while Maulus Shane had not achieved soccer celebrity status he had had success in business. He was counted amongst the rich in the land. Until everything had sunk like a mansion built on a sinkhole. The hole had been his character, or the lack thereof; the same trait that also proved to be the eventual bane of the soccer whizzes and quickly eroded their wealth when they hit the sunset of their career. So while he enjoyed the limelight, least did he project his latter days as a withered, sickly, crushed and penniless specimen of broken humanity.

Old man Maulus was roused from his unhappy contemplation when the ball hit him on the cheek on a bounce from the head of the boy. The sudden impact stunned him and made him to totter like a weak-rooted tree in a breeze. The ball fell at his feet and rolled to a stop against a stone close by. Walking past Maulus to retrieve the ball, the boy approached him to offer apologies. But he did not understand what the boy was saying. Instead he held out the slip of paper with the address to the handsome face of the remorseful youth. The boy took the paper from him and looked at it for a while. Then he said politely "Please, follow me" and moved ahead in the direction to his left, eager to atone for his accidental transgression through service to his victim.

With the first few steps of following the boy Maulus was seized in a spasm of coughing. At the sound of the throaty noise the boy turned round to look at the old man, and saw the flow of blood-red mucus gushing through his mouth and nose as he was bent double. Revolted, the boy placed the slip of paper on the ground, placing a stone over it to ensure it would not be blown away, and quickly fled the scene. Tuberculosis was a dreaded highly transmissible disease, the victims of which were avoided like the plague.

Soon the seizure abated. He straightened up and with his shoe kicked sand to cover the unpleasant ooze. He took some few steps to where the boy had placed the paper and retrieved it from under the stone. Then he continued like a zombie in the direction where the boy had been leading him. A while later he was overtaken by a woman. She turned to look at him when she had outpaced him by some yards, her curiosity needing to be satisfied. When their eyes met Maulus beckoned to her and extended the creased and dirty paper towards her. She walked back and took the slip, read it and concluded that he needed guidance to that address. Maulus avoided speaking for fear it would trigger another bout of coughing, and pretended not to hear when the woman asked him where he had come from. All he wanted was to be taken to the place where his son lived in apparent comfort and luxury.

Now that he knew he was near his destination Maulus dreaded the meeting, but he had come too far to retreat. Perhaps he should have stayed in his hometown and died in due course; after all death was as predictable as night followed day. As William Shakespeare wisely philosophized in his book 'Julius Caesar':

"Cowards die many times before their death;
The valiant never tastes of death but once.
Of all the wonders that I yet have heard,

It seems to me most strange that men should fear;
Seeing that death, a necessary end,
Will come when it will come."

But the normal human instinct was such that man would avoid death at all cost, if possible, even at the eleventh hour in the execution chamber. Those people who committed suicide were the exception rather than the rule; the rare few on the path of aberration that baffled the sanity of humanity.

Come to think of it, it was likely that he could end up himself in the execution chamber; he was currently on bail awaiting trial for three murders. Too late now he regretted the folly of his actions: criminals ultimately met their day of reckoning. No matter how crafty the criminal, and how supposedly foolproof the crime, there was bound to be a hitch. And that had been the case with him, after so many years had gone by. Nemesis was hot at his heels, and he kept tripping at every turn.

But for now he needed to locate the house of the son, and the woman was the chaperon to take him there, like Christopher Columbus on a discovery expedition to the New World.

The woman patiently kept in step with him. The house was right on the street, and after what seemed like a long walk they stood before the imposing edifice. She crosschecked the number on the gate to that on the tortured slip of paper, and returned it to Maulus who slipped it deep into his pocket like some treasured gem.

"This is the place," the woman said and made to move on her way. Maulus mumbled a "thank you" and waved to her. She turned back to look at him pityingly, waving back. Her hand could have been a flag flapping in the wind as she kept waving until she turned a corner and disappeared out of sight. In the Republic of Zollara the aged were respected to the point of veneration; a virtue drilled into the psyche of the youth from infancy.

Maulus Shane stood behind the gate, awed by his surroundings. He looked like an outcast behind the gate of heaven; a beggarly figure totally out of synch in the chic environs. He had heard that his son had made it in the city against all odds, but he could not imagine he had made it so big as to live in a mansion that could pass for a castle. Lifting up his head he could see the house rising three floors high. The building was enclosed by a concrete wall some seven feet high, and topped with electrified mesh all the way round. The tops of the two metal gates spotted sharp spikes and were of equal height with the wall.

In the cities of the Republic of Zollara the rich lived in homes designed to offer great safeguard against armed robbers. In effect they lived in a state of self-imposed incarceration in edifices comparable to maximum- and medium-security prisons. The gangs of armed robbers were as ruthless as they were greedy, and they were often on the prowl for victims. They epitomized the biblical picture portrayed in the gospel of John chapter 10 verse 10: *"The thief cometh not, but for to steal, and to kill, and to destroy."* They struck when least expected, so potential targets went to great extent to protect themselves and their families.

So it transpired that while Maulus Shane stood hesitantly behind the gate, the electronic monitors in the various rooms in the house were flashing red to indicate the presence of a stranger. The residents of the house carried deactivating gadgets so the monitors did not light up when they were behind the gate. Simultaneously, the ever alert guard bulldog had scented an unfamiliar presence at the gate and started barking in frenzy without let up.

Dreams and Nightmares
(https://www.createspace.com/4476359)

Synopsis:

This book contains 101 easy to read poems aimed at making poetry an enjoyable and stimulating experience. It takes the reader on a jolly journey of poetry exploration and discovery. Poetry can be a hobby for all rather than being the preserve of academia. Those who are not used to poetry will find this book a good basis for cultivating love for poetry.

Some poems in the book are reproduced below:

Discontent
(The myth of the greener grass)

You wake up startled

By the shriek of the alarm gadget,

It is still early and you're drowsy

You wish you could sleep on

But duty beckons in a world

Crazy with the hustle and bustle

Of making living a worthwhile gamble.

Your next wish is to call-in sick,

But the bills keep mushrooming

In a soil fetile with needs and trifles

Whilst the per-hour pay rate is a mite.

You must punch-in promptly at 5.00 a.m.

But it's a whole hour's travel

By bus and train and by foot

To get to that place of drudgery

Where the taskmaster of a boss

Reigns supreme like a despot.

Makes you wonder which is better:

This humdrum life of survival or death?

So you question the why of your birth

Or why you were not born to privilege

With a path of succession from the womb

To riches, thrones, and even dictatorships

Like those you see and envy

On the other side of the fence.

If you but lived on the other side

Perhaps you might appreciate that

"All that glitters is not gold,"

And that some base metals

Reflect more light than raw gold.

You may be the gold in the ore

Discontent at this stage will conceal you

Whilst you can shine through optimism

At whatever status or stage you're in life.

Whispers
(On experiencing love through nature)

Much more endearing

Purrs of tenderness

Unspoken words of impassioned tenor

Soothing echoes all year long

Lullabies to unborn babies

Calm to my strained nerves

Drowsiness to my agitated soul

Cloud nine in my earthly domicile

Embrace to my loneliness

Whispers of love

I hear throughout nature:

In the forest by the gurgling stream,

In the chirping of birds,

In the murmuring of winds,

In the pitter-patter of raindrops,

In the rustle of leaves,

In the splash of sea waves,

Even in the boom of thunder;

These are the restorative moments

That I treasure and long for.

The Cry of the Beloved
(On the pain of wars and terrorism)

A world in turmoil of

Man's hatred for man,

Man at war with man

Killing and plundering

On the battlefields of cities,

In offices and at homes,

At the malls and on the streets,

At the theatres and casinos,

Even on nursery school grounds.

The extremists on airplanes,

The snipers in vans and on rooftops,

Tanks spitting fire on civil protestors,

Guns blazing in non-combat zones,

Missiles exploding over serene skies,

Bombing 'crafts hovering

Like hungry predatory hawks

After human-prey chickens.

The devilish suicide bombers,

The AK-47 armed lunatic on the loose

Bullets spewing like sprinklers on flowers,

And Chemical weapons showering like rain.

Images of the terrorist and the terrorized,

The kidnapper and the kidnapped,

Testimonials to man's inhumanity to man

Sadistic manifestos cunningly crafted

 And incubated in the human DNA.

Viral vitriolic dispersal of mayhem

Like poisoned granules

Whizzed about in a tempest.

Amidst all the man-made turmoil

The haunting heartbreak

Is the cry of the beloved,

The victimized beloved in pain

And the impotence of a lover to help.

Bad Guys Good Guy-
The Carjackers (Series 1)

Synopsis:

A gang of highway robbers, the bad guys in society, is hell bent on escapades of carjacking, killing and mayhem. It takes one good guy who is a victim to the gang to bring the bunch of hooligans to its heels. How does this one amateurish guy face up to the hardened specialized bad guys? For the answer you are about to embark on a roller coaster of rollicking thrill on the trails of death and mayhem, in the style of classic Hadley Chase novels.

Chapter One (extract):

From where he stood in the valley Sparky Spearman looked up onto the hills. He saw a figure outstretch itself and leap through the air in a movement suggestive of the gliding of a hawk. As he stepped aside the attacker's leg in the air lashed out and made contact with his face. He stumbled, missed a step and fell backwards. As he got up he reeled from a stunning impact to his head from the palm of the attacker, huge with solid calloused fingers. Sparky staggered backwards, recovered and surging forward unleashed a frantic left-handed shot. The attacker avoided contact with a deft sideways step. A forceful punch to Sparky's stomach sent him lurching to fall backwards. The attacker rushed over and seizing him by the throat demanded in a guttural voice: "Where's the bag? I'll kill you if you don't tell."

"It's ...ssss...ssss......" Sparky tried to speak, but pretended that the hold on his neck made speech difficult. The attacker relaxed his grip for the words to come out. That was when Sparky jerked up his right knee and connected with the groin of the attacker. As the stunned adversary spun back Sparky kicked out with the right leg, caught him in the rib and sent him crashing to the ground.

Up again on their feet almost immediately both antagonists approached each other with cautious, calculating steps. They were like two cunning boxers, each seeking to deliver the knockout punch.

Sparky was the first to deliver a misdirected heavy fisted blow that the opponent had no difficulty in avoiding. The attacker countered with a well-aimed forceful shot to Sparky's chest, followed with a boxer-style uppercut to the cheek. Sparky's face etched in convulsed agony. Blindly, he threw a fist which the attacker gripped and in a spin sent him spiraling to a shuddering thud on the rocks.

The attacker broke into cries of victory, and advanced menacingly towards Sparky as he lay on the ground.

"Once again, for the last time," he raged, "tell me where you've hidden the bag, or I'll bash your head against the rocks." He stooped to take hold of Sparky by the head.

With a swift movement Sparky rolled over. When the attacker's hands touched the ground where his head had been, Sparky grabbed him by his hand and pulled. The assailant fell flat on the ground, with his forehead smashing against a rock. He remained prone in a state of semi-consciousness. Sparky lifted himself off the ground, walked over to the comatose man, raised him up by the shoulders and banged him down hard on the rocky terrain. Then he collapsed in a heap of exhaustion by the side of his enemy.

When Sparky came to an hour or so later, the aggressor still lay the way he had fallen, and had not as much as moved an inch. Standing over the now immobilized attacker Sparky attempted to lift him up, but he was of no mean weight. He bent on his knees, grabbed the comatose man at the waist and managed with much exertion to lift him up over his head. Grunting, Sparky strained to haul himself up into a standing position. He felt that if the ground was soft it would break up and swallow him and the load he carried like a house on a sinkhole. He took some few steps forward to the edge of the swift flowing river. With a heave he flung his load into the swirling river. "Bad guy with stone bad weight," he muttered, feeling relieved of being rid of his burden. He watched it instantly carried along the course of flow, but within some few yards it got wedged between two rocks in the river, trapped by the bulky head. He soon realized that throwing the body into the river had been an impulsive useless act: he ought to have left it on the battleground for when law enforcement would come to retrieve it. He hoped that the gridlock would hold the body in place in the water until then. He sat on on a rock by the edge of the river and scooped water with his cupped hands to wash his face. He repeated the process over and over until he felt refreshed and clear headed. Then he drank mouthfuls of the water till his stomach bellyached.

Spasms of hunger stirred up within him: he had not eaten in the past twenty four hours before he and his murdered companion had been waylaid by the band of highway pirates, of which the dead attacker had belonged.

When Sparky turned round he halted in his tracks, as if the blood circulating within him had frozen. He was staring into the steel barrel of an AK-47. The mean-looking gangster he had escaped from earlier on the highway had his fingers inching towards the trigger. His blood-shot eyes seemed to be rotating in their sockets like the evil flashing tongue of the venomous viper about to strike. He kept advancing towards Sparky, one measured step at a time. He seemed to derive strength from sheer malice, and the fear he saw etched on the face of Sparky.

For Sparky it was veritable doomsday. He braced himself for the impact of the slugs that would launch him backwards to fall into the river dead.

earlier on the highway had his fingers inching towards the trigger. His blood-shot eyes seemed to be rotating in their sockets like the evil flashing tongue of the venomous viper about to strike. He kept advancing towards Sparky, one measured step at a time. He seemed to derive strength from sheer malice, and the fear he saw etched on the face of Sparky.

For sparky it was veritable doomsday. He braced himself for the impact of the slugs that would launch him backwards to fall into the river dead.

Academic Papers by the author
(On the web at http://www.oboulo.com)

- Re-engineering the Dysfunctional Business to be a good fit with the Organizational Ecosystem.

- An Analysis of the Book "The Tao Of Leadership

- A Business Plan for a Concrete Products Plant.

- Organizations as Organisms and Cultures and their Implications for Leadership

I trust you've had an enjoyable reading excursion through the pages of this book.

About the Author

Chrys lives in Alexandria in Virginia after periods of stay in Ghana and Santa Barbara in California. He studied at the University of Ghana for a B.Sc. in Accounting. He graduated with a master's degree in Organizational Management from Antioch University in Santa Barbara. His working career covers years as Cost Accountant at Nestle Ghana and Finance Officer at the President's Special Initiative for Distance Learning in Ghana. He also served in the position of Director of Accounting at The Samarkand Retirement Community in Santa Barbara, California.

His books include the novels *'Life's Twists and Turns'* and *'Muddy Waters.'* Editions of the books have been published by Tate Publishing.

He is working on a thriller series titled *'Bad Guys Good Guy.'*

Chrys is married to Helena. The couple has four sons: Valery, Hilary, Emery and Larry.

Made in the USA
San Bernardino, CA
24 September 2017